THE AMAZING TITLE PAGE OF DOOM!
I Was a Teenage Hallucination #3

WRITTEN IN TWO CHAPTERS, THE DEAD LIVE, AND THE FUTURE IS HERE AND HERE IS THE FUTURE.

I WAS A TEENAGE HALLUCINATION!
3

I Was a Teenage Hallucination # 3

Copyright 2007 All Rights Reserved. ISBN 978-0-6151-8490-6

DANGER! IDEAS HAVE CONSEQUENCE! THIS COMIC BOOK IS NOT INTENDED FOR ANYONE UNWILLING OR UNABLE TO TAKE RESPONSIBILITY FOR THEIR OWN MENTAL STATES AND THE RESULTS OF THEIR ACTIONS!

THIS COMIC BOOK IS FURTHER NOT INTENDED FOR ANYONE WHO IS UNABLE OR UNWILLING TO DIFFERENTIATE BETWEEN OBJECTIVE AND SUBJECTIVE REALITY!

THE IDEAS AND OPINIONS EXPRESSED IN THIS COMIC BOOK ARE ENTIRELY THOSE OF THE FICTIONAL CHARACTERS PORTRAYED THEREIN AND DO NOT IN ANY WAY REFLECT THE IDEAS OR OPINIONS OF THE CREATOR, PUBLISHER, OR ANYONE ASSOCIATED WITH THE CREATOR OR PUBLISHER IN ANY WAY. ALL CHARACTERS PORTRAYED IN THIS COMIC BOOK ARE COMPLETELY FICTIONAL IN SPITE OF ANY RESEMBLANCE TO ANY PERSONS LIVING, DEAD, OR MYTHOPOEIC. THE CREATOR OF THIS COMIC BOOK IS ALSO COMPLETELY FICTIONAL AND BEARS NO RESEMBLANCE TO ANY PERSON LIVING, DEAD, OR MYTHOPOEIC. WE APOLOGIZE FOR ANY CONFUSION THIS MAY CAUSE ANY PERSONS, LIVING, DEAD, OR MYTHOPOEIC. BUT THROUGH SAID APOLOGY NO LIABILITY OR RESPONSIBILITY IS EITHER INTENDED OR IMPLIED. PLEASE PLAY NICELY AND REMEMBER TO SHARE. THIS CONCLUDES OUR BROADCAST! NO ONE CAN HELP YOU IF YOU DON'T HELP YOURSELF!

Copyright 2007 All Rights Reserved. ISBN 978-0-6151-8490-6

NOW THAT YOU HAVE SEEN, YOU MUST SHOW OTHERS! HERES HOW...

STEP 1: Using your vast Powers go to http://stores.lulu.com/iwasateenagehallucinationthestore **DO IT NOW!**

STEP 2: Utilizing your Mighty Cursor click on the VOLUME OF CHOICE, REMEMBER THERE ARE 3.

STEP 3: You may now view the details and Preview the Books if that's what youre Into. Its your trip.

STEP 4: select the Add Print to Cart option.

STEP 5: Complete the purchase info. Pay close attention to what Shipping Option meets your needs best!

Purchase as many copies as you can! Your Very Existence depends upon it!

AND THEN THE SECOND ANGEL WAS REPLACED BY THE THIRD ANGEL!

THEN THE FOURTH ANGEL APPEARED.

"MY BELOVED, I HAVE COME TO SHARE THE MYSTERY OF EXISTENCE WITH YOU! BEFORE ANYTHING IS THE DREAMER. WHEN SLEEP FALLS UPON HUMANS AND ALL THINGS VANISH, EVEN THEIR SELVES, THE UNSPEAKABLE STATE IS COMPARABLE TO THE DREAMER. THE DREAMER IS UNMANIFEST EXISTENCE, ULTIMATE TRANSCENDENCE!"

THEN THE MIGHTY VISION OCCURRED! E SEEMED TO FLOAT IN A SEA OF STARS AND SHE APPEARED!

"THEN THREE STATES ARISE AS A RESULT OF AN IMPULSE TOWARD MANIFESTATION WHICH OCCURS WITHIN THE DREAMER. THE FIRST STATE IS OBJECTLESS AWARENESS, ITS TENDENCY IS TO LOOSE ITSELF AGAIN WITHIN TRANSCENDENCE. THE SECOND STATE IS UNALTERABLE EXISTENCE, ITS TENDENCY IS TO MAINTAIN THE IMPULSE TOWARD MANIFESTATION. THE THIRD STATE IS UNENDING JOY, ITS TENDENCY IS TO COALESCE EXPERIENCE. THESE THREE STATES ARE QUALITIES OF THE DREAM, MANIFEST EXISTENCE. AND THE STATES ARE CALLED NEGATIVE MANIFEST EXISTENCE. THE DREAMER AND THE DREAM ARE NOT SEPARATE, TO ACCOMPLISH THE PURPOSE BEYOND."

SHE EXPLAINED THE SECRET OF LIFE!

"THE DREAM IS ULTIMATELY THE IMPULSE TOWARD MANIFESTATION AND IS NOT SEPARATE FROM THE DREAMER. THE DREAM IS ALSO ALL MANIFEST EXISTENCE AND IS ULTIMATE IMMANENCE! NEGATIVE MANIFEST EXISTENCE IS NOT CALLED NEGATIVE BECAUSE IT IS BAD OR DEFICIENT BUT BECAUSE IT IS A LATENT STATE OF MANIFEST EXISTENCE WHEREAS LATER STATES ARE CONSIDERED BLATANT. WITHIN THE STATE OF UNENDING JOY THE COALESCENT TENDENCY CONTAINS THE POTENTIAL MANIFESTATIONS OF THE IMPULSE TOWARD MANIFESTATION WITHIN BLATANT EXISTENCE. THESE POTENCIES ARE THE BLUEPRINT AND PATTERN AROUND WHICH ALL SUBSEQUENT EXISTENCE IS FORMED FITTINGLY THESE POTENCIES ARE CALLED POTENTIAL EXISTENCE."

"THE COALESCENT TENDENCY THEN ACTUALIZES FOUR STATES, THE STATE OF EXPANSION, THE STATE OF CONTRACTION, AND THE STATES OF HARMONY AND COMPLETION. POTENTIAL EXISTENCE THEN ACTUALIZES WITHIN EACH STATE... SEQUENTIALLY FORMING VARIOUS PROCESSES EXPRESSIVE OF THE IMPULSE TOWARD MANIFESTATION. THE SUMMATION OF THESE PROCESSES IS WHAT IS PERCEIVED IN NATURE AS CONSCIOUS AND UNCONSCIOUS AWARENESS WITH THE POTENTIAL OF INVOLVEMENT WITH THE WHOLE OF EXISTENCE. THIS SUMMATION ARISES TO FULFILL THE PROCESSES IN THE FOUR STATES."

AND THEN JOINING THESE MONSTERS FROM BELOW NATURE ARRIVED DEMONS AND SHADES OF EVIL WHO CONSUMED HUMANS ALIVE!

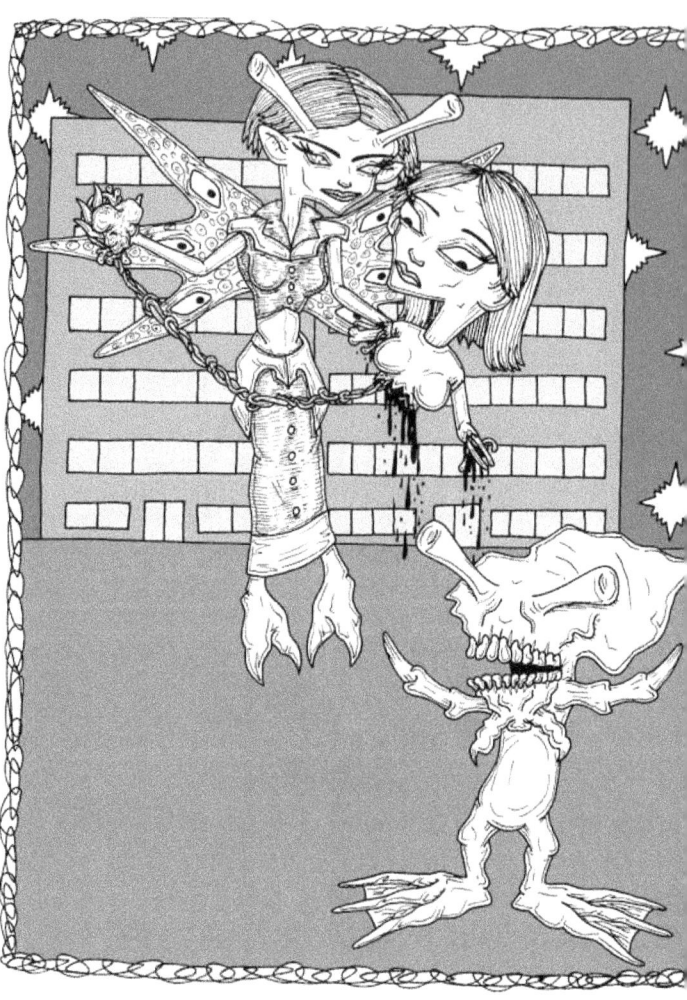

THEN, RAVING FROM THE DARKNESS, SCREAMING INTO NATURES PLANES, THE SUM TOTAL OF CHAOS ARRIVED, ITS BIRTHRIGHT TO CLAIM!

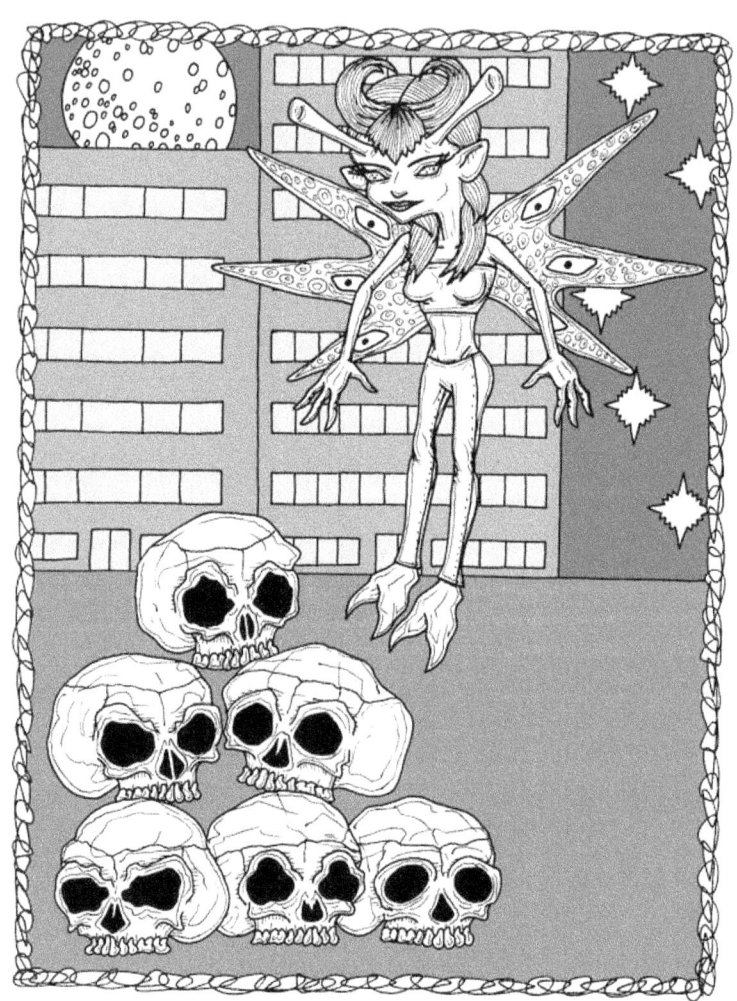

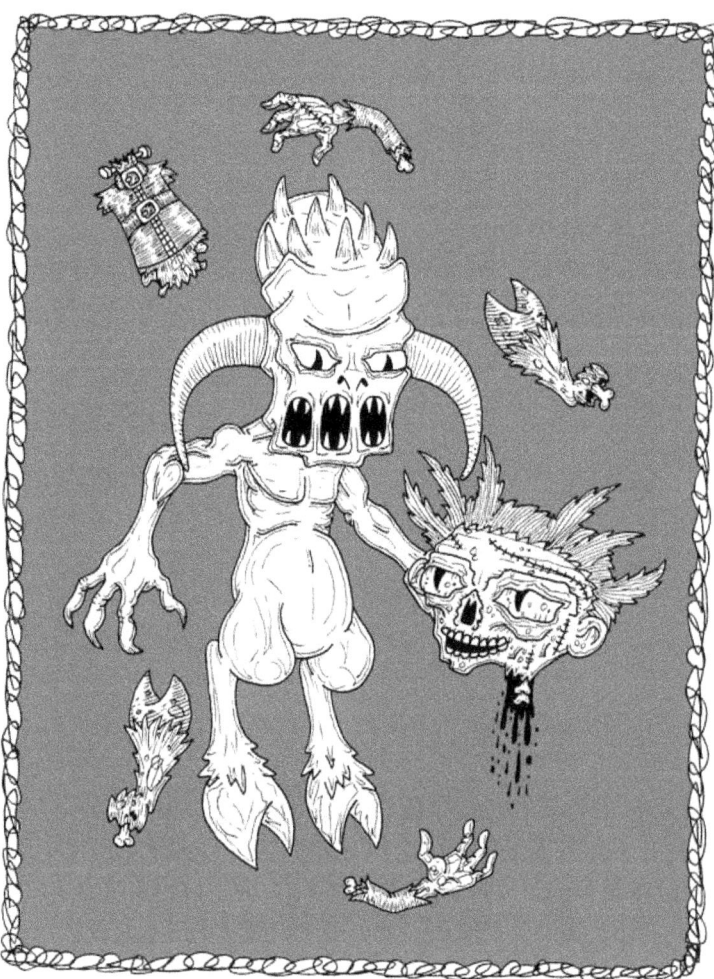

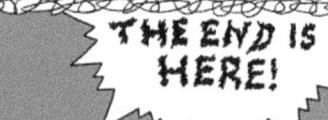

An I Was a Teenage Hallucination Poster

An I Was a Teenage Hallucination Poster

www.ingramcontent.com/pod-product-compliance
Ingram Content Group UK Ltd.
Pitfield, Milton Keynes, MK11 3LW, UK
UKHW050415240426
12048UKWH00020B/1520